ED YOUNG

Night Visitors

PHILOMEL BOOKS • NEW YORK

Library of Congress Cataloging-in-Publication Data
Young, Ed. Night visitors / Ed Young   p.   cm.   Summary: Retelling of a Chinese
folktale in which a young scholar learns respect for all forms of life when he becomes
part of an ant colony in a dream. [1. Folklore—China.]   I. Title.
PZ8.1.Y84Ni   1995   398.2'0951—dc20   [E]   94-33355   CIP   AC
I S B N   0 - 3 9 9 - 2 2 7 3 1 - 8

10 9 8 7 6 5 4 3 2 1

First Impression

AUTHOR'S NOTE

Night Visitors is a retelling of a Chinese folk
tale inspired by two versions. The better-
known version is the *Nang Ko Journal*, written
during the T'ang Dynasty. The name and
place of this retelling, however, came from
an excerpt called "The Ants," from *Tai-shang
Kan-yin Pien*, part of which dates back to
the sixth century B.C.

LONG, LONG AGO in a small village in southern China there lived a
young scholar called Ho Kuan, who was both gentle and strong, and
who lived peacefully alone with his mother and father. Then one day
ants invaded the family's rice storehouse and ate and stole their grain.

Angry, Ho's father shouted at a servant, "Trace the ants to their nest and drown them!"

"No, Father," Ho pleaded. "Seal the walls and floor so tight no ant can enter! That way, no harm will come to ant or grain."

Ho's father turned his back. "I give you one month to seal the floors and walls. If you fail, I will flood the storehouse."

That night Ho Kuan stayed up late poring over his books, searching for a way to seal the storehouse so tight no ant could enter.

Then, at midnight he was startled by the loud sounds of drums and bells outside in the courtyard.

Looking out his window, Ho saw soldiers in shining black armor entering the house gates. An officer standing next to a black carriage bowed and announced: "His Majesty summons Ho Kuan to his palace!"

His Majesty? The palace? What Majesty? What palace? Ho was puzzled. But, both honored and curious, he took leave of his parents and entered the mysterious black carriage.

For days, Ho followed the black-armored soldiers

across wide plains and rivers, through thick forests.

Finally, amongst the fragrance of flowers, they arrived at the foot of a great mountain city. Never had Ho Kuan seen such beautiful architecture, such friendly crowds of people.

As Ho climbed the palace stairs, the king rose from his throne to receive him, saying, "Welcome to our city, Ho Kuan. You are my guest for as long as you please."

For many days Ho Kuan stayed in the strange and beautiful city, and was accepted by all. So impressed was the king with his kindness and character that he gave his only daughter in marriage to the young Ho.

To Ho his new wife was as gentle and beautiful as the morning mist, and they spent many days together in a small chamber of their own.

Ho Kuan had never been happier.

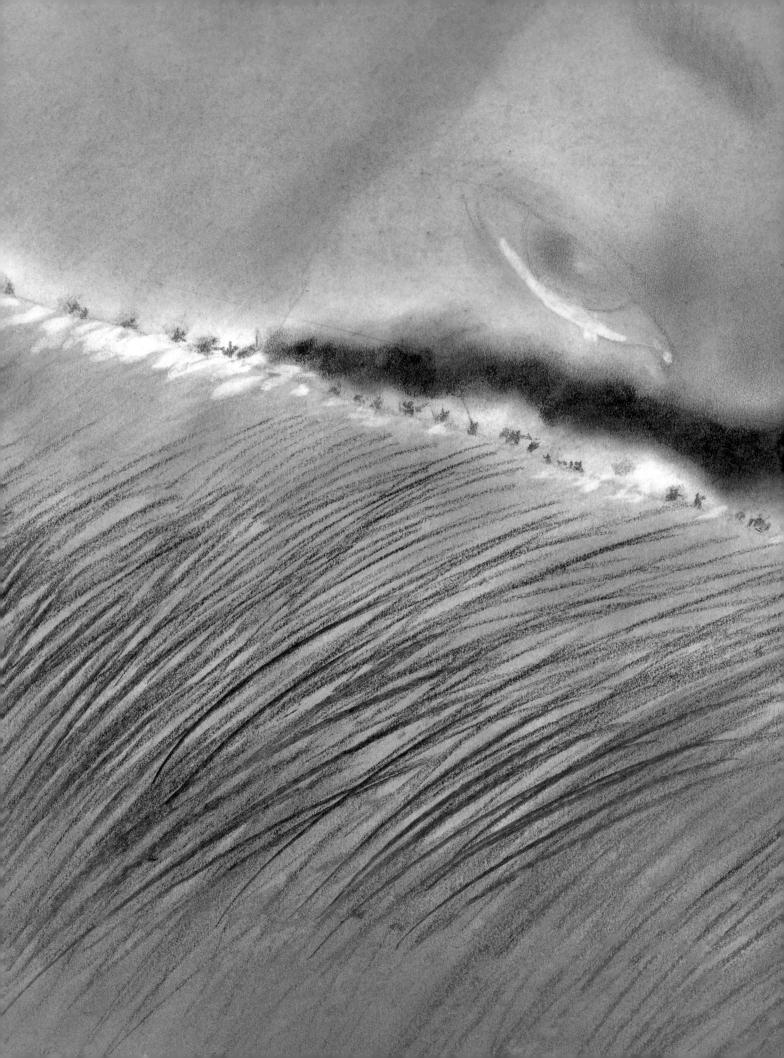

But their days together were too few. One day, warriors in red armor attacked their countryside. They were greater in number and stronger. "If we do not stop them, they will destroy us," the king told Ho in tears.

The next day, the red warriors ambushed a royal envoy and killed Ho's beloved wife and her attendants.

Though Ho was a man of peace, this was an invasion he had to stop. Skilled in martial arts and clever in strategies, he trained the king's army, and finally drove the red invaders from the country.

But, although the Kingdom had its peace, Ho Kuan could not forget his dear wife. He realized that it was time for him to return to his native home.

The king came to him before he left. "I shall miss you, Ho Kuan," he said, "for you have become one of my family, but I respect what you must do." The king sent Ho Kuan with a royal escort, and told him that he would find a token of his kingdom's gratitude under a cassia tree at his parents' home.

With drums and bells of the escort still in his ears, Ho Kuan woke to find himself at his own desk with his books still in front of him. "Ah, then, it has all been a dream," he consoled himself.

Then, across his papers, he saw a line of ants.

He followed them out of the house,
down a slope, up a mound, winding
through grasses, across a small stream.

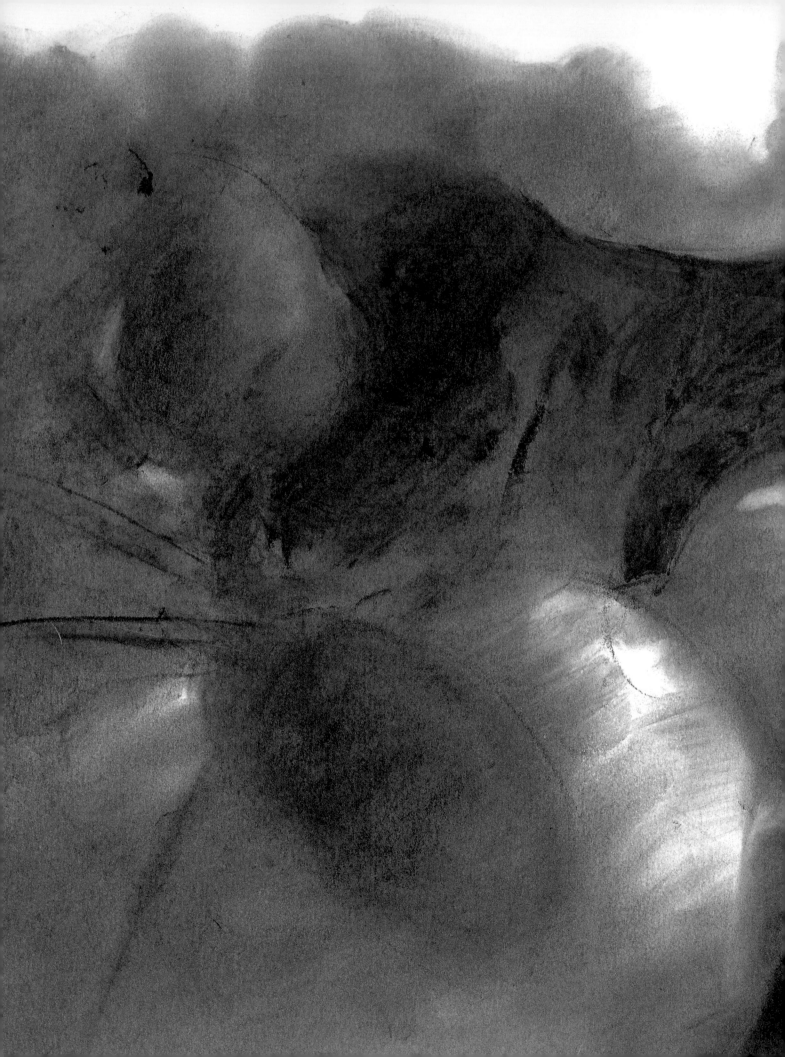

Among the fragrance of flowers, he came to what seemed to be a palace of many steps upon which sat a majestic black ant. Next to it was a small chamber.

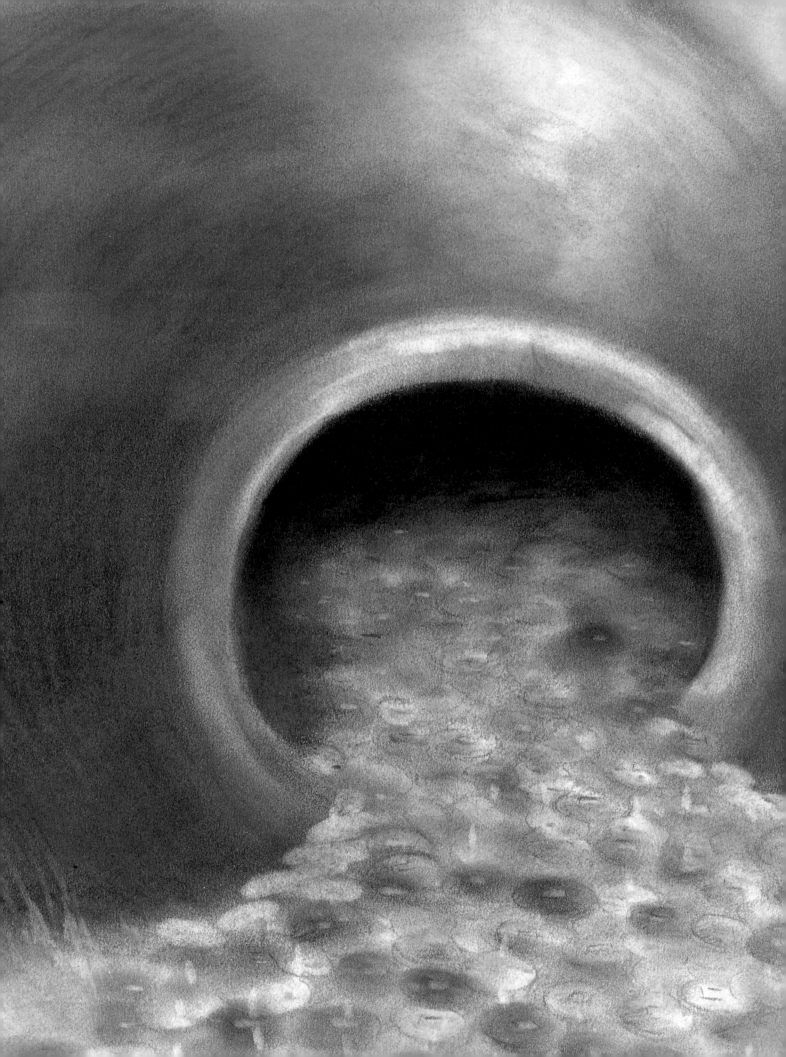

He was, he realized, at the hollow of a cassia tree. And there he discovered a great earthen jar. When he picked it up, old silver coins poured out.

Ho Kuan used the treasure to seal the walls and floors of the storehouse, and for the rest of his life, to all who would listen, he taught respect for all forms of life, no matter how small.

To Saint Francis, who opened
us to all forms of life,
and
C. G. Jung, who made us open
to our subconscious self.